LOVE AND INFORMATION

by Caryl Churchill

Cast
Nikki Amuka-Bird
Linda Bassett
Scarlett Brookes
Amanda Drew
Susan Engel
Laura Elphinstone
John Heffernan
Joshua James
Paul Jesson
Billy Matthews
Justin Salinger
Amit Shah
Rhashan Stone
Nell Williams
Josh Williams
Sarah Woodward

Director James Macdonald
Set Designer Miriam Buether
Costume Designer Laura Hopkins
Lighting Designer Peter Mumford
Sound Designer Christopher Shutt
Casting Director Amy Ball
Assistant Director Caitlin McLeod
Production Manager Paul Handley
Stage Manager Laura Draper
Deputy Stage Manager Fran O'Donnell
Assistant Stage Manager George Cook
Stage Management Work Placement Maia Alvarez Stratford
Costume Supervisor Jackie Orton
Musical Director Simon Deacon
Choreographer Stuart Hopps
Dialect Coach Majella Hurley
Set Built by Miraculous Engineering Ltd
Scenic Painter Kerry Jarrett

The Royal Court and Stage Management wish to thank the following for their help with this production: Almeida Theatre, Donmar Warehouse, Radmilla Mileusnic, National Youth Theatre, Steven Rose, Mark Salter, Rocky Shahan, Dr Hannah Stockton.

THE COMPANY

CARYL CHURCHILL (Writer)

FOR THE ROYAL COURT: Seven Jewish Children, Drunk Enough to Say I Love You?, A Number, Far Away, This is a Chair, Blue Heart, Mad Forest, Ice Cream, Serious Money, Fen, Top Girls, Cloud Nine, Traps, Light Shining in Buckinghamshire, Owners.

OTHER THEATRE INCLUDES: The Skriker (National).

MUSIC THEATRE INCLUDES: Lives of the Great Poisoners, Hotel (both with Orlando Gough).

Caryl has also written for radio and television.

NIKKI AMUKA-BIRD

THEATRE INCLUDES: The Trial of Ubu (Hampstead); Welcome to Thebes (National); Doubt (Tricycle); Twelfth Night (Bristol Old Vic); World Music (Donmar); A Midsummer Night's Dream, The Tempest, The Servant of Two Masters (RSC); Top Girls, 50 Revolutions (Oxford Stage Company).

TV INCLUDES: Sinbad, Luther, Survivors, Small Island, Silent Witness, The No. I Ladies Detective Agency, Torchwood, The Last Enemy, Whistleblower, Five Days, Born Equal, Shoot the Messenger, Robin Hood, Spooks, Crime Monologues: Grace, The Line of Beauty, Afterlife, Murder Prevention, The Canterbury Tales: Man of Law's Tale, NCS Manhunt, Always Be Closing, Forgive and Forget, Safe as Houses, Grafters.

FILM INCLUDES: Coriolanus, The Disappeared, The Omen, Cargo, Almost Heaven.

RADIO INCLUDES: Noughts & Crosses, Charity, The Man in Black, The Lucky Girl, White Shoes, Charity, England, The Colour Purple, Mister Pip, Free Juice For All, The No. I Ladies Detective Agency, Top Girls, Lady Play, Troilus And Cressida.

LINDA BASSETT

FOR THE ROYAL COURT: In Basildon, Wastwater, The Stone, Lucky Dog, Far Away (& Albery); East is East (with Tamasha Theatre Company & Birmingham Rep & Stratford East/Duke of York's); The Recruiting Officer, Our Country's Good (& Garrick); Serious Money (& Wyndham's & Public, NY); Aunt Dan and Lemon (& Public); Abel's Sister, Fen (with Joint Stock & UK Tour & Public).

OTHER THEATRE INCLUDES: The Road to Mecca (Arcola); A Winter's Tale, Pericles, Henry IV Parts I & II, The Theban Plays, Artists and Admirers (RSC); Phaedra (Donmar); Hortensia & The Museum of Dreams (Finborough); Love Me Tonight, The Awakening (Hampstead); Richard III, The Taming of the Shrew (Globe); John Gabriel Borkman (ETC); Out in the Open (Birmingham/Hampstead); Five Kinds of Silence (Lyric Hammersmith); The Dove (Croydon Warehouse); The Triumph of Love (Almeida/UK tour); The Clearing (Bush); Schism in England, Juno and the Paycock, A Place with the Pigs (National); The Seagull (Liverpool Playhouse); George Dandin, Medea, Woyceck, Bald Prima Donna (Leicester Haymarket/Liverpool Playhouse/Almeida); The Cherry Orchard (Leicester Haymarket); Falkland Sound (Belgrade Theatre Studio); Belgrade T.I.E Company (Coventry); Interplay Theatre Company (Leeds).

TV INCLUDES: The Spies of Warsaw, The Life and Adventures of Nicholas Nickleby, Grandma's House, Lark Rise to Candleford, Sense and Sensibility, This Little Life, Our Mutual Friend, Far from the Madding Crowd, Silent Film, Kavanagh Q. C., Casualty, Christmas, A Touch of Frost, Dinner Ladies, Love Hurts, A Small Dance, No Bananas, EastEnders, Say Hello to the Real Dr. Snide, The Bill, Newshounds, A Village Affair, Bramwell, Loved Up, Cold Light of Day, Frank Stubbs Promotes, Skallagrig.

FILM INCLUDES: Effie, West is West, Cass, The Reader, Kinky Boots, Separate Lies, Spivs, Calendar Girls, The Last Time, The Hours, The Martins, East is East, Beautiful People, Oscar and Lucinda, Mary Reilly, Waiting for the Moon, Indian Summer.

RADIO INCLUDES: Notes to Self, The Memory of Water, Freefall, Abishag the Virgin.

SCARLETT BROOKES

Scarlett graduated from RADA in 2012. Love and Information is Scarlett's professional stage debut.

RADIO INCLUDES: Dracula.

MIRIAM BUETHER (Set Designer)

FOR THE ROYAL COURT: Get Santa!, Sucker Punch, Cock (& New York), Relocated, The Wonderful World of Dissocia (& EIF), My Child.

OTHER THEATRE INCLUDES: Chariots of Fire (Hampstead/West End); Decade (Headlong); Wild Swans, The Government Inspector, In the Red and Brown Water, The Good Soul of Szechuan, Generations (Young Vic); Earthquakes in London (National); Judgement Day (Almeida); King Lear (New York); Six Characters in Search of an Author (Chichester/West End/Sydney); The Bacchae, Realism (National Theatre of Scotland/EIF); The Bee (Young Vic/Japan); Guantanamo Honor Bound to Defend Freedom (Tricycle/West End/New York/San Francisco).

OPERA INCLUDES: Anna Nicole, Il Trittico – Suor Angelica (ROH); Carmen (Salzburg Festival); Turandot (ENO); The Death of Klinghoffer (Edinburgh Festival/Scottish Opera); The Sacrifice (WNO).

AWARDS INCLUDE: Evening Standard Award 2010 for Best Design for Earthquakes in London and Sucker Punch, Hospital Club Creative Award for Theatre 2008; Critics Award for Theatre in Scotland 2004/5, Linbury Prize 1999.

AMANDA DREW

FOR THE ROYAL COURT: Enron (& West End), The Stone, Faces in the Crowd, The Ugly One, Mr Kolpert, The Man of Mode, The Libertine.

OTHER THEATRE INCLUDES: A Streetcar Named Desire (Everyman, Liverpool); Butley (Duchess); House of Games, Parlour Song, A Chain Play, Enemies, Doña Rosita the Spinster (Almeida); Otherwise Engaged (Criterion); Blithe Spirit (Theatre Royal, Bath/UK tour/West End); Play (BAC); 100 (Australia/ Brazil tour); Damages (Bush); Madame Bovary: Breakfast With Emma, The House of Bernarda Alba (Shared Experience); Eastward, Ho!, The Malcontent, The Roman Actor, Jubilee, Love in a Wood (RSC); Top Girls (New Vic); The School of Night (Chichester); Twelfth Night, John Gabriel Borkman, Hove (National).

TV INCLUDES: Silent Witness, Switch, Midsomer Murders, Holby Blue, EastEnders, Golden Hour, M.I.T, No Angels, The Bill, Men Behaving Badly, Tough Love.

FILM INCLUDES: Anonymous, Elfie Hopkins & The Gammons, Jerusalem, The Other Man, Mrs Dalloway.

AWARDS INCLUDE: Best Supporting Actress 2003 – Clarence Derwent Award for Eastward, Ho!

LAURA ELPHINSTONE

FOR THE ROYAL COURT: Breathing Corpses, Country Music.

THEATRE INCLUDES: Utopia (Soho/Live, Newcastle); Chalet Lines (Bush); Top Girls (Chichester/Trafalgar Studios); A Month in the Country (Chichester); Marine Parade (Brighton Festival); Pains of Youth, Women of Troy (National); Bedroom Farce (West Yorkshire Playhouse); Far from the Madding Crowd (ETT tour); Glass Eels (Hampstead); Heatbreak House (Watford Palace); Scenes from an Execution (Hackney Empire); Tom and Viv (Almeida); The Crucible (RSC/West End); Pictures of Clay (Royal Exchange).

TV INCLUDES: Doctors, My So Called Life Sentence, Tess of the d'Urbervilles.

FILM INCLUDES: The History Boys.

RADIO INCLUDES: Interviews, Hard Road, Cooking With Stanley.

SUSAN ENGEL

FOR THE ROYAL COURT: Spinning Into Butter, The Happy Haven, Hotel In Amsterdam, Macbeth.

OTHER THEATRE INCLUDES: The Crucible (Regent's Park); Dido, Queen of Carthage, Her Naked Skin, The Hour We Knew Nothing of Each Other, Angels in America, Watch on the Rhine, Spring Awakening (National); Richard III, King Lear, The Good Person of Sichuan (National & UK tour); Women Beware Women, Luminosity, Bad Weather, The Dybbuk, King John, The Tempest, The Comedy of Errors, Julius Caesar, Henry IV Part II, The Wars of the Roses (RSC); Cousin Vladimir (RSC/West End); Hecuba (Donmar); Hamlet (Donmar/West End); Brand (Haymarket); A Passage to India (Nottingham Playhouse/tour); After the Gods, The Ascent of Mount Fuji, Shortlist (Hampstead); The Sea (Chichester); Prayers of Sherkin (Old Vic); An Inspector Calls, Footfalls (Garrick); Clandestine Marriage (West End/UK tour); Himself (Nuffield); The Cherry Orchard (Leicester/West End): A Kind of Alaska (Duchess); Last of the Red Hot Lovers (Criterion); Private Life of the Third Reich (Open Space).

TV INCLUDES: The Café, Midsomer Murders, Afterlife, The Black Death, Dalziel & Pascoe, Trial & Retribution, Tuesday the 12th, The Vice, Kavanagh Q.C., Underworld, Inspector Morse, Doctor Who.

FILM INCLUDES: The Magic Seed, The Leading Man, Damage, Anastasia, Ascendancy, Butley, King Lear.

RADIO INCLUDES: Bombs on Aunt Dainty, Pilgrim, Doctor Who, Miss Balcombe's Orchard, The View From Here: Israel, Flaw in the Motor, Dust in the Blood, Pilgrim 2, The Play's the Thing: Proud Songster, Dropping Bombs, Left At The Angel, The January Wedding, The Making of the English Escape, The Great Pursuit, The Bruno Bettelheim Project, The Raj Quartet, The Lumber Bomber, Miss Esther's Guest, Are You Sure?, Peeling Figs For Julius, Moving On, I Will Tell, Le Grande Therese, Anne of Green Gables, Black Narcissus, The Christmas Collection, Hamlet.

AWARDS INCLUDE: Clarence Derwent Award for Best Supporting Actress.

JOHN HEFFERNAN

THEATRE INCLUDES: The Physicists (Donmar); She Stoops to Conquer, Emperor and Galilean, After the Dance, The Habit of Art, The Revenger's Tragedy, Major Barbara (National); The Last of the Duchess (Hampstead); Richard II (Tobacco Factory); Love, Love, Love (Paines Plough); Carrie's War (West End); King Lear, The Seagull, King John, Romeo and Juliet, Much Ado About Nothing (RSC); Lloyd George Knew My Father (Richmond & tour); Hamlet (English Touring); Five Finger Exercise (Frankfurt International); Western (Edinburgh Fringe/Wimbledon/Live, Newcastle); A Midsummer Night's Dream (Haymarket).

TV INCLUDES: Henry IV Parts I and II, The Shadow Line, Casualty 1909, Holby Blue.

FILM INCLUDES: Having You, King Lear.

RADIO INCLUDES: Shakespeare's Restless World, The Archers.

LAURA HOPKINS (Costume Designer)

COSTUME DESIGN INCLUDES: Beautiful Burnout (UK tour); A Delicate Balance (Hampstead); Rudolf, Musical (Vienna); Sinatra (Palladium/tour).

THEATRE DESIGN INCLUDES: Troilus and Cressida (RSC/Wooster Group); Soul Sister (Hackney Empire/Savoy/UK tour); A Midsummer Night's Dream, Ragtime (Regent's Park); You Can't Take It With You (Royal Exchange); The Death of Klinghoffer (ENO/Metropolitan Opera); Juliet and her Romeo (Bristol Old Vic); Shoes (Sadler's Wells/Peacock); King Lear (Chile); Lullaby and Gross Indecency (Duckie); Black Watch, Peter Pan, The House of Bernarda Alba (National Theatre Scotland); Kellerman, Hotel Methuselah (Imitating The Dog tour); Time and the Conways (National); Rough Crossings (Headlong); Faustus (Royal & Derngate); Hamlet, Othello (Royal & Derngate/UK tour); Skåne (Hampstead); The Merchant of Venice (RSC); Peer Gynt (Guthrie Theatre); Golden Ass, Macbeth, Storm (Globe); Adolf Hitler: My Part in His Downfall (UK tour); The INS Broadcasting Unit (ICA); Così fan tutte, Falstaff (ENO); Falstaff (Opera North); Jerusalem, Mister Heracles (West Yorkshire Playhouse); Elixir of Love (New Zealand Opera); Swan Lake Re-mixed (Volksoper, Vienna); The Rake's Progress (Welsh National Opera).

AWARDS INCLUDE: TMA Best Design for Faustus (Royal & Derngate).

JOSHUA JAMES

James graduated from RADA in 2012. Love and Information is James's professional stage debut.

TV INCLUDES: Whites, Silent Witness, Identity.

FILM INCLUDES: Summer in February.

PAUL JESSON

FOR THE ROYAL COURT: Cock, The Seagull, A Lie of the Mind, The Normal Heart (& West End), Deadlines (with Joint Stock), Falkland Sound/Voces de Malvinas, Marie and Bruce, Bingo.

OTHER THEATRE INCLUDES: Travelling Light, Mary Stuart, The Devil's Disciple, Hamlet, Ghetto, Hedda Gabler, The Changeling, Cat on a Hot Tin Roof (National); Hamlet, Henry VIII, Bingo, The Tempest, Antony and Cleopatra, The Winter's Tale, A Jovial Crew, The Beggar's Opera, Richard II, Two Shakespearean Actors, Troilus and Cressida (RSC); King Lear, Twelfth Night (Donmar/New York); The Winter's Tale, The Cherry Orchard (Old Vic/New York); Awake and Sing!, King Lear, Hedda Gabler, Mrs Gauguin (Almeida); Death of a Salesman (Royal Lyceum, Edinburgh); Troilus and Cressida, The Seagull (Edinburgh Festival); The Winter's Tale (Shakespeare's Globe); Rita, Sue and Bob Too, A State Affair (Out of Joint); The Flight into Egypt, Slavs!, Goose-Pimples (also West End); Comings and Going (Hampstead); Three Sisters (Greenwich); Deadlines, The House (Joint Stock); Mary Stuart, The Graduate, Dreaming (West End).

RECENT TV INCLUDES: Margaret, Midsomer Murders, The Devil's Whore, Foyle's War, The Amazing Mrs Pritchard, Slave Trader, Spooks, Rome, Danielle Cable, The Glass.

FILM INCLUDES: Closed, Wall, Closer to the Moon, Coriolanus, Vera Drake, All or Nothing, The Ploughman's Lunch.

AWARDS INCLUDE: 1986 Olivier Award for Outstanding Performance of the Year in a Supporting Role, for The Normal Heart.

JAMES MACDONALD (Director)

FOR THE ROYAL COURT: Cock (& Duke Theater, New York), Drunk Enough to Say I Love You?, Dying City, Fewer Emergencies, Lucky Dog, Blood, Blasted, 4.48 Psychosis (& European/US tours), Hard Fruit, Real Classy Affair, Cleansed, Bailegangaire, Harry and Me, Simpatico, Blasted, Peaches, Thyestes, The Terrible Voice of Satan.

OTHER THEATRE INCLUDES: King Lear, The Book of Grace, Drunk Enough to Say I Love You? (The Public Theater, New York); Top Girls (Broadway/Manhattan Theatre Club); Dying City (Lincoln Center); A Number (New York Theatre Workshop); And No More Shall We Part (Hampstead/Traverse); A Delicate Balance, Judgment Day, The Triumph of Love (Almeida); John Gabriel Borkman (Abbey/BAM); Dido Queen of Carthage, The Hour We Knew Nothing of Each Other, Exiles (National); Glengarry Glen Ross (West End); Troilus und Cressida, Die Kopien (Berlin Schaubühne); 4.48 Psychose (Vienna Burgtheater); The Tempest, Roberto Zucco (RSC); Love's Labour's Lost, Richard II (Royal Exchange); The Rivals (Nottingham Playhouse); The Crackwalker (Gate, Notting Hill); The Seagull (Crucible); Miss Julie (Oldham Coliseum); Juno and the Paycock, Ice Cream and Hot Fudge, Romeo and Juliet, Fool for Love, Savage/Love, Master Harold and the Boys (Contact); Prem (BAC/Soho Poly).

OPERA INCLUDES: A Ring, A Lamp, A Thing (Linbury, ROH); Eugene Onegin, Rigoletto (Welsh National Opera); Die Zauberflöte (Garsington); Wolf Club Village, Night Banquet (Almeida Opera); Oedipus Rex, Survivor from Warsaw (Royal Exchange/Hallé); Lives of the Great Poisoners (Second Stride).

FILM INCLUDES: A Number.

Associate Director of the Royal Court from 1992–2006. NESTA fellow 2003–06.

BILLY MATTHEWS

Love and Information is Billy's professional stage debut.

TELEVISION INCLUDES: Harry Enfield and Paul Whitehouse Sketch Show, Henry IV Parts I & II, One Night, New Tricks.

CAITLIN MCLEOD

AS AN ASSISTANT DIRECTOR FOR THE ROYAL COURT: Love, Love, Love, In Basildon, Haunted Child.

OTHER THEATRE DIRECTION INCLUDES: And I And Silence, Northern Star (Finborough); Slaughter City (RSC, rehearsed reading); The Lady's Not For Burning, Elephant's Graveyard (Warwick Arts Centre Studio); Seven Jewish Children (Capital Centre).

OTHER ASSISTANT DIRECTION INCLUDES: Hamlet (Globe); The Talented Mr Ripley (Royal & Derngate); Touched (North Wall, Oxford).

Caitlin is the Trainee Director at the Royal Court.

PETER MUMFORD (Lighting Designer)

FOR THE ROYAL COURT: Jumpy, Our Private Life, Sucker Punch, Cock, The Seagull, Drunk Enough to Say I Love You?, Dying City (& set design).

OTHER THEATRE INCLUDES: Top Hat, Absent Friends, Much Ado About Nothing, The Lion in Winter, The Misanthrope, An Ideal Husband, Carousel, Fiddler on the Roof (West End); Betrayal (Crucible); The Last of the Duchess (Hampstead); Testament (Dublin Theatre Festival); A Streetcar Named Desire (Guthrie, Minneapolis); Heartbreak House (Chichester); Pictures from an Exhibition (Young Vic); Parlour Song, Hedda Gabler, Cloud Nine (Almeida); Scenes from an Execution, All's Well That Ends Well, The Hothouse, Exiles (National).

OPERA & DANCE INCLUDES: The Damnation of Faust, Lucrezia Borgia, Elegy for Young Lovers, Punch and Judy (Geneva); Bluebeard's Castle, Madam Butterfly (ENO); Faster, $E=MC^2$ (Birmingham Royal Ballet); Pelleas and Melisande (Mariinsky); The Soldier's Tale (Chicago Symphony); Madame Butterfly, Faust, Carmen, Peter Grimes, 125th Gala (New York Met); Eugene Onegin (LA Opera/ROH); Passion (Minnesota Opera); La Cenerentola (Glyndebourne); Carmen (also set design), Petrushka (Scottish Ballet); Il Trovatore (Paris); Fidelio, Two Widows, Don Giovanni, The Ring (Scottish Opera); The Midsummer Marriage (Chicago Lyric Opera); The Bartered Bride (ROH). Currently directing/designing a concert version of The Ring Cycle for Opera North.

AWARDS INCLUDE: 1995 Olivier Award for Outstanding Achievement in Dance for The Glass Blew In (Siobhan Davies) and Fearful Symmetries (Royal Ballet), 2003 Olivier Lighting Award for The Bacchai (National). Knight of Illumination Award 2010 for Sucker Punch at the Royal Court.

JUSTIN SALINGER

FOR THE ROYAL COURT: Bliss, The Food Chain, Under the Blue Sky.

OTHER THEATRE INCLUDES: The Physicists, Privates on Parade (Donmar); The Homecoming (RSC); Beauty and the Beast, The Cat in the Hat, Our Class, The Seagull, Pillars of the Community, UN Inspector, A Dream Play, Iphigenia at Aulis, Peter Pan, Chips with Everything, Dealer's Choice (National); Through a Glass Darkly, Doña Rosita the Spinster (Almeida); Pressure Drop (On Theatre/Wellcome Collection); Nocturnal, Candide (Gate, Notting Hill); The Birthday Party (Lyric, Hammersmith); King of Hearts (Out of Joint); Modern Dance For Beginners, Jump Mr Malinoff, Jump (Soho); Kick For Touch, The Unthinkable (Crucible); The Backroom (Bush); Perpetua (Birmingham Rep); Much Ado About Nothing (Cheek by Jowl).

TV INCLUDES: Being Human, Casualty, New Tricks, He Kills Coppers, Doc Martin, Whistleblowers, Empathy, Beau Brummell, The Line of Beauty, Foyle's War, The Bill, Hitler: The Rise of Evil, Trust,

Murphy's Law, Waking the Dead, Offenders, The Great Dome Robbery, The Vice, Dark Realm, London's Burning.

FILM INCLUDES: Creature, Heartless, The Calling, Daylight Robbery, Enduring Love, Revengers Tragedy, Peaches, Velvet Goldmine.

AMIT SHAH

FOR THE ROYAL COURT: Rough Cuts: The Spiral, Shades, Free Outgoing.

OTHER THEATRE INCLUDES: The Comedy of Errors, The Hour We Knew Nothing of Each Other, Odyssey, The Man of Mode, The Alchemist, The Life of Galileo, The Royal Hunt of the Sun (National); King Lear (Donmar); Arabian Nights (RSC); A Christmas Carol (Rose, Kingston); The Hot Zone (Lyric, Hammersmith); Twelfth Night (Albery); Bombay Dreams (West End).

TV INCLUDES: Le Grand, Fresh Meat, White Van Man, Black Mirror: National Anthem; Whites, Hustle, Ingenious, Casualty, Benidorm, The Palace, Honest, Lead Balloon, Afternoon Play: Are You Jim's Wife?, Life Begins.

FILM INCLUDES: Guinea Pigs, The Infidel, Lost Paradise, It's a Wonderful Afterlife, 13 Semesters, Like Minds, The Blue Tower.

CHRISTOPHER SHUTT (Sound Designer)

FOR THE ROYAL COURT: Kin, Aunt Dan and Lemon, Serious Money, Road.

OTHER THEATRE INCLUDES: The Last of the Haussmans, The Comedy of Errors, Emperor and Galileo, White Guard, Coram Boy, A Dream Play, Mourning Becomes Electra, Humble Boy, Play Without Words, Albert Speer, Not About Nightingales, Machinal (National); Burnt by the Sun, Every Good Boy Deserves Favour, Gethsemane, Happy Days (National/tour); War Horse (National/West End/Broadway); Nocturnal (Gate); A Disappearing Number, The Elephant Vanishes, Mnemonic, Street of Crocodiles, Three Lives of Lucie Cabrol (Complicite); The Tempest, The Comedy of Errors, Twelfth Night, King Lear, Much Ado About Nothing, King John, Romeo and Juliet (RSC); All My Sons, The Resistible Rise of Arturo Ui (New York); Bacchae, Little Otik (National Theatre Scotland); Playboy of the Western World, A Moon for the Misbegotten, All About My Mother (Old Vic); School for Scandal, Julius Caesar (Barbican); Philadelphia, Here I Come!, Prince of Homburg, Piaf, The Man Who Had All The Luck (Donmar); Ruined, Judgment Day (Almeida); Far Away, Coram Boy (Bristol Old Vic); Bacchae/Blood Wedding, Beyond the Horizon/Spring Storm (Royal & Derngate).

RADIO INCLUDES: Shropshire Lad, Tennyson's Maud, After the Quake, Mnemonic, A Disappearing Number.

AWARDS INCLUDE: Tony Award for War Horse.

RHASHAN STONE

FOR THE ROYAL COURT: Clubland

OTHER THEATRE INCLUDES: Trance (Bush); Southwark Fair, The Red Balloon, Sweeney Todd (National); Simply Heavenly (Young Vic/Trafalgar Studios); The Inland Sea (Oxford Stage Company); Henry VI parts I,II,III, Richard III, Hamlet, Camino Real, Much Ado About Nothing (RSC); A Funny Thing Happened on the Way to the Forum, The Merry Wives of Windsor (Regent's Park); The Tempest, Present Laughter, The Seagull (West Yorkshire Playhouse); As You Like It (Cheek By Jowl/tour); Animal Crackers (Royal Exchange); Happy End (Nottingham Playhouse); Chasing The Moment (NT Studio/BAC /Pleasance); Five Guys Named Moe (West End).

TV INCLUDES: Strikeback, City Hall, Silk, Black Mirror, Episodes, Land Girls, The Lucy Montgomery Show, The Armstrong & Miller Show, Taking the Flak, Mutual Friends, Outnumbered, Bike Squad, Casualty, Love Soup, Perfect Day, Bodies, The Crouches, The Bill, Fifteen Storeys High, Holby City, Picking up the Pieces, The Detectives, Goodnight Sweetheart, Desmond's.

FILM INCLUDES: Three And Out, Wondrous Oblivion, Blind Date.

JOSH WILLIAMS

FOR THE ROYAL COURT: Our Private Life.

OTHER THEATRE INCLUDES: Shivered, Arlo (Southwark); Lord of the Flies (Regent's Park).

TV INCLUDES: Mayday.

NELL WILLIAMS

Love and Information is Nell's professional stage debut.

TV INCLUDES: Loving Hiss Hatto, The Revolting World of Stanley Brown.

SARAH WOODWARD

FOR THE ROYAL COURT: Jumpy, Presence, Built on Sand.

OTHER THEATRE INCLUDES: The Cherry Orchard, The Hour We Knew Nothing of Each Other, Present Laughter, Wild Oats, The Sea (National); Snake in the Grass (The Print Room); The Merry Wives of Windsor (Globe/US tour); Judgment Day (Almeida); Rookery Nook (Menier Chocolate Factory); Macbeth, A Midsummer Night's Dream, Romeo and Juliet, Arms and the Man (Regent's Park); The Comedy of Errors, Much Ado About Nothing (Globe); Woman in Mind (Salisbury Playhouse); Les Liaisons Dangereuses (Playhouse); The Real Thing (Donmar/West End/Broadway); Tom and Clem (West End); Habeus Corpus (Donmar); The Tempest, Love Labour's Lost, The Venetian Twins, Murder in the Cathedral, Henry V, Camille, Hamlet, Richard III, Red Noses (RSC); London Assurance (Chichester/West End); Artist Descending a Staircase (King's Head/West End); The Rape of Lucrece (Almeida); Angleus, From Morning Till Night (Soho Poly); Talk of the Devil (Bristol Old Vic); The Winter's Tale (Birmingham Rep).

FILM INCLUDES: Bright Young Things, I Capture the Castle, Doctor Sleep, The House of Angelo.

TV INCLUDES: Loving Miss Hatto, The Politician's Husband, DCI Banks: Aftermath, Law & Order, Kingdom, Hear the Silence, Final Demand, Doctors, The Bill, Casualty, Gems, Poirot, New Tricks.

AWARDS INCLUDE: Best Supporting Actress, Olivier Awards 1998 for Tom and Clem, Shakespeare's Globe Classic Award, 1993 for The Tempest, Clarence Derwent Award 1988 for Artist Descending a Staircase.

THE ENGLISH STAGE COMPANY AT THE ROYAL COURT THEATRE

'For me the theatre is really a religion or way of life. You must decide what you feel the world is about and what you want to say about it, so that everything in the theatre you work in is saying the same thing ... A theatre must have a recognisable attitude. It will have one, whether you like it or not.'

George Devine, first artistic director of the English Stage Company: notes for an unwritten book.

photo: Stephen Cummiskey

As Britain's leading national company dedicated to new work, the Royal Court Theatre produces new plays of the highest quality, working with writers from all backgrounds, and addressing the problems and possibilities of our time.

"The Royal Court has been at the centre of British cultural life for the past 50 years, an engine room for new writing and constantly transforming the theatrical culture." Stephen Daldry

Since its foundation in 1956, the Royal Court has presented premieres by almost every leading contemporary British playwright, from John Osborne's Look Back in Anger to Caryl Churchill's A Number and Tom Stoppard's Rock 'n' Roll. Just some of the other writers to have chosen the Royal Court to premiere their work include Edward Albee, John Arden, Richard Bean, Samuel Beckett, Edward Bond, Leo Butler, Jez Butterworth, Martin Crimp, Ariel Dorfman, Stella Feehily, Christopher Hampton, David Hare, Eugène Ionesco, Ann Jellicoe, Terry Johnson, Sarah Kane, David Mamet, Martin McDonagh, Conor McPherson, Joe Penhall, Lucy Prebble, Mark Ravenhill, Simon Stephens, Wole Soyinka, Polly Stenham, David Storey, Debbie Tucker Green, Arnold Wesker and Roy Williams.

"It is risky to miss a production there." Financial Times

In addition to its full-scale productions, the Royal Court also facilitates international work at a grass roots level, developing exchanges which bring young writers to Britain and sending British writers, actors and directors to work with artists around the world. The research and play development arm of the Royal Court Theatre, The Studio, finds the most exciting and diverse range of new voices in the UK. The Studio runs play-writing groups including the Young Writers Programme, Critical Mass for black, Asian and minority ethnic writers and the biennial Young Writers Festival. For further information, go to www.royalcourttheatre.com/playwriting/the-studio.

"Yes, the Royal Court is on a roll. Yes, Dominic Cooke has just the genius and kick that this venue needs... It's fist-bitingly exciting." Independent

Autumn 2012

Jerwood Theatre Downstairs

6 Sept – 13 Oct

love and information by Caryl Churchill

In this fast moving kaleidoscope more than a hundred characters try to make sense of what they know.

25 Oct – 24 Nov

NSFW by Lucy Kirkwood

A sharp new comedy looking at power games and privacy in the media and beyond.

6 Dec – 19 Jan

in the republic of happiness by Martin Crimp

A provocative roll-call of contemporary obsessions.

Jerwood Theatre Upstairs

18 Oct – 17 Nov

the river by Jez Butterworth

The writer and director behind *Jerusalem* return with a bewitching new story.

23 Nov – 22 Dec

hero by E. V. Crowe

A bracing new story of a heroic modern man. *Hero* is part of the Royal Court's Jerwood New Playwrights programme, supported by the Jerwood Charitable Foundation.

Royal Court Theatre Productions and Ambassador Theatre Group present
Royal Court at the Duke of York's

Until 3 Nov

jumpy
by April De Angelis

Tamsin Greig reprises her critically acclaimed role in this frank and funny family drama.

9 Nov – 5 Jan

constellations
by Nick Payne

Sally Hawkins and Rafe Spall perform in this explosive new play about freewill and friendship.

Duke of York's Theatre, St Martin's Lane, WC2N 4BG

020 7565 5000
www.royalcourttheatre.com

Sloane Square ⚡ Victoria 🄴 royalcourt 🄵 theroyalcourttheatre

Principal Sponsor **Coutts**

ARTS COUNCIL ENGLAND

ROYAL COURT SUPPORTERS

The Royal Court has significant and longstanding relationships with many organisations and individuals who provide vital support. It is this support that makes possible its unique playwriting and audience development programmes.

Coutts is the Principal Sponsor of the Royal Court. The Genesis Foundation supports the Royal Court's work with International Playwrights. Theatre Local is sponsored by Bloomberg. The Jerwood Charitable Foundation supports new plays by playwrights through the Jerwood New Playwrights series. The Andrew Lloyd Webber Foundation supports the Royal Court's Studio, which aims to seek out, nurture and support emerging playwrights. Over the past ten years the BBC has supported the Gerald Chapman Fund for directors.

The Harold Pinter Playwright's Award is given annually by his widow, Lady Antonia Fraser, to support a new commission at the Royal Court.

PUBLIC FUNDING
Arts Council England, London
British Council
European Commission Representation in the UK

CHARITABLE DONATIONS
Martin Bowley Charitable Trust
Gerald Chapman Fund
Columbia Foundation
Cowley Charitable Trust
The Dorset Foundation
The John Ellerman Foundation
The Eranda Foundation
Genesis Foundation
J Paul Getty Jnr Charitable Trust
The Golden Bottle Trust
The Haberdashers' Company
Paul Hamlyn Foundation
Jerwood Charitable Foundation
Marina Kleinwort Charitable Trust
The Andrew Lloyd Webber Foundation
John Lyon's Charity
The Andrew W Mellon Foundation
The David & Elaine Potter Foundation
Rose Foundation
Royal Victoria Hall Foundation
The Dr Mortimer & Theresa Sackler Foundation
John Thaw Foundation
The Vandervell Foundation
The Garfield Weston Foundation

CORPORATE SUPPORTERS & SPONSORS
BBC
Bloomberg
Coutts
Ecosse Films
Kudos Film & Television
MAC
Moët & Chandon
Oakley Capital Limited
Smythson of Bond Street
White Light Ltd

BUSINESS ASSOCIATES, MEMBERS & BENEFACTORS
Auerbach & Steele Opticians
Bank of America Merrill Lynch
Hugo Boss
Lazard
Louis Vuitton
Oberon Books
Peter Jones
Savills
Vanity Fair

DEVELOPMENT ADVOCATES
John Ayton MBE
Elizabeth Bandeen
Kinvara Balfour
Anthony Burton CBE
Piers Butler
Sindy Caplan
Sarah Chappatte
Cas Donald (Vice Chair)
Celeste Fenichel
Emma Marsh (Chair)
Deborah Shaw Marquardt (Vice Chair)
Sian Westerman
Nick Wheeler
Daniel Winterfeldt

Supported by
ARTS COUNCIL ENGLAND

LOVE AND INFORMATION

Caryl Churchill

Note on Text

The sections should be played in the order given but the scenes can be played in any order within each section.

There are random scenes, see at the end, which can happen any time.

The characters are different in every scene. The only possible exception to this are the random Depression scenes, which could be the same two people, or the same depressed person with different others.

This text went to press before the end of rehearsals and so may differ slightly from the play as performed.

1

SECRET

Please please tell me

no

please because I'll never

don't ask don't ask

I'll never tell

no

no matter what

it's not

I'd die before I told

it's not you telling, even if you didn't

I wouldn't

it's you knowing it's too awful I can't

but tell me

no

because if you don't there's this secret between us

stop it

if there's this secret we're not

please

we're not close any more we can't ever

but nobody knows everything about

yes but a big secret like this

it's not such a big

then tell me

will you stop

it's big because you won't tell me

no I won't.

Is it something you've

don't start guessing

or something you want to

please

or you've seen or heard or know or

please

and if it's something you've done is it a crime or a sin or just embarrassing because whichever

no I don't want you to know.

All right.

All right I'll tell you

you don't have to

I'll tell you

yes tell me because I'll never

it's not that

tell me because I'll always

all right I'm telling you.

Tells in a whisper.

No

yes

no

I warned you

but that's

yes

oh no that's

yes

how could you

I did.

Now what? now what? now what?

CENSUS

Why do they need to know all this stuff?

They're doing research. It guides their policy. They use it to help people.

They use it to sell us things we don't want.

No that's the people who phone up. I don't answer any of their questions, I just say No thank you, there's no need to swear at them.

I've made a mess of it now anyway.

You'll get into trouble if you don't do it.

They won't know.

They know you exist.

FAN

Love him so much

love him more than you

I'd jump out of the window

eat fire

cut off my hand

eat dogshit

kill my mother

eat catfood

yeuch

just to touch him

just to tell him

just to see him

just to have him see me.

He was born at ten past two in the morning and I was born at two past ten

how do you know?

Mum says

two past ten

she said just after ten so that's two

that isn't two

it is two

anyway he was born on Tuesday and I was born on Wednesday and you were only born on Friday

that's stupid.

His favourite colour's blue

favourite food's chilli

favourite animal's snakes

favourite holiday was in Bermuda

what's his favourite smell?

Roses

you're making that up

well what?

I'm asking you

you don't know

I'm asking you

you don't know do you go on tell me

you tell me

I don't know you tell me

all right I don't know so we've got to find out

you mean neither of us know?

It's all right we'll find out

I can't believe neither of us

it's in here somewhere

I know I used to know

wait

is it chicken?

wait

you can't find it

I can't

you're not looking properly

I can't find it

here let me

you can't find it

wait

it's not there

wait

see you can't.

What are we going to do?

we've got to know

I won't be able to sleep

what are we going to do?

TORTURE

He's wearing me out.

Take a break.

Do you want to go in?

I'll give him a cigarette.

He's not ready to talk.

I thought we'd got there yesterday.

I thought we'd got there yesterday but he's past that.

He'll get to where he'll say anything.

We're not paid extra for it to be true.

I'll give him a cigarette while you have a cigarette and I'll tell him you'll be back.

LAB

So we hatch a batch of eggs in the lab

and where do you get the

from the poultry breeders who supply them to the battery

oh the intensive

yes or some of them might go to farms but either way

so either way they're going to be

yes by twelve weeks they'll be plucked and lying on their backs

in a supermarket

on your table

so you're not taking the life

I am taking the life

but even if you didn't they'd be

they wouldn't live to be old chickens, no.

So you've got the chickens and

about a day old, fluffy yellow like little Easter

and you do some experiment on them?

what we do is we get them to peck

because chicks do peck a lot

they peck at everything and what we do is we get them to peck beads that have been dipped either in water or some stuff that tastes bitter

not poison

no it makes them wipe their beaks on the floor then they're fine again and of course we're writing all this down which chick which bead and how many pecks and then my colleague injects this tiny amount of very slightly radioactive liquid into each side of the chick's brain so

oh no stop

I know but they don't seem at all

it doesn't hurt

they don't show any

ok so what's it for? it's going to show up something in their brains

because what we've injected has a sugar in it that gets used by the nerve cells and the more sugar is taken up the more brain activity and the radioactivity acts as a tracer like in a scanner so you can measure that and see exactly where in the brain the sugar

and the idea is it's different in the different

what we hope to see you see is that it's different

depending on what they've learned about the

yes because we give them the beads again and they have learned because the ones who had the beads with water come back and peck it again and the ones

they won't peck it

the ones that had the bitter bead have learned not to peck it

that's terrific.

But that's not what we're finding out, what we're finding out

changes in the brain

exactly, what changes in the brain correspond to that memory

so to do that you have to

yes I hold the bird in my left hand and quickly cut off its head with a big pair of scissors

aah

and I drop the body in a bucket and take the head and peel back the skin and cut round the skull and there's the brain

there's the brain

so I put it in a dish of ice and my colleague cuts it into slabs with a razor blade and then he dissects out tiny samples that he puts into test tubes and they're immediately frozen while meanwhile I'm taking the brain out of the next chick

yes

and that's what I do.

And then you analyse

yes and there is a substantial increase

so you can measure

and not just the increase but exactly where because if you slice

slice the brain

slice the frozen brain into thin sections and put them on slides you get pictures

you can see

you can see exactly depending on how dark and you can convert it into false colour which of course looks

prettier

prettier yes and easier to read though the information is the same

which is

that the learning takes place on the left side of the brain

and you can see

and there's another version where you stain the sample with silver salts and then you can count the new spines on the dendrites which are

yes the little tiny

because at that degree of magnification a thumbnail would be two hundred and fifty metres wide

so you can see the memory

yes you can see the actual changes

see what the chick learnt about the bead.

SLEEP

I can't sleep.

Hot milk.

I hate it now.

Book?

I haven't got one I like.

Just lie there and breathe.

My head's too full of stuff. Are you asleep?

No no, what, it's fine. You can't sleep?

I think I'll get up and go on Facebook.

REMOTE

You don't seem to have a tv.

There used to be one but it stopped working. The reception's no good anyhow.

I brought my laptop.

You might have a reception problem there.

It's not that I need it. There's no phone signal is there?

You'd have to go to town. Or I think someone said there's a spot about two miles up the road if you go down towards the cliff and stand on a rock, you'd have to know it.

We can listen to the radio. Does it work?

I did warn you.

I know.

It's quiet here.

I like it quiet.

You can always cycle down and get a newspaper.

It's all right.

I don't have time you see.

Don't you sometimes want a weather forecast?

I want you to be happy here.

I am happy here.

You'll find you can feel if it's raining.

2

IRRATIONAL

Is an irrational number real?

It's real to me.

But can you have an irrational number of oranges?

Not as things stand, no.

I'm not comfortable with the whole idea.

There was someone called Hippasus in Greek times who found out about the diagonal of a square and they drowned him because no one wanted to know about things like that.

Like what?

Numbers that make you uncomfortable and don't relate to oranges.

I can see how they might want to do that.

Drown him?

Maybe he should have kept quiet about it if he knew they couldn't stand it.

Is that what you do?

AFFAIR

I don't know if I should tell you.

What?

But you're my friend more than she is.

What is it?

What do you think yourself? is it better to know things or not to know things? Is it better just to let things be the way you think they are, the way they are really because if someone tells you something that might change everything and do you want that? Do you think it's interfering or is it what a friend ought to do?

You're going to have to tell me now, you know that.

But some people might say you shouldn't say anything because you might not want to hear anything against your best friend but I do keep seeing them together and last night I was having a drink with her after work and he just sort of turned up and after a bit they left together, they hardly bothered to come up with a story, I just wondered. I'm probably imagining things and I shouldn't put ideas into your head because it may all be perfectly all right, I'm sorry maybe I should have kept quiet, oh dear, I've told you now.

They're having an affair.

They are? you know that? you knew that?

I've known that quite a while.

How long?

Three years.

And you're ok with it?

Yes it's all ok. Thanks though.

MOTHER

While Mum's out

what?

I've something to tell you

ok

so you need to look at me

I'm listening

I need to feel you're really paying attention

I can pay attention and do other things at the same time, I'm not brain-dead, I can see and hear and everything

will you listen?

I'm listening, fuck off. Is this going to take long?

Don't pay attention then, I'm just telling you, you might like to know Mum's not your mother, I'm your mother, Mum's your nan, ok? Did you listen to that?

Does Mum know you're telling me?

I just decided.

Are we going to tell her you told me?

I don't know. Do you think?

Why didn't she say before, she doesn't want me to know, she's going to go crazy

it'll be ok

it's not my fault, she can't blame me for knowing

it'll be ok, I'll tell her I told you, it's my fault.

How old were you, wait, thirteen. You were thirteen? Thirteen.

Yes, that's why.

It's probably better than not being born.

That's what I thought, I thought you'd like to be born.

Who's my dad then?

I didn't see him any more, he went to a different school. He was twelve.

I don't think I feel like you're my mum though. I don't have a sister, I don't like that. Do you want me to feel different about you?

I just didn't want it to be something I could never say.

I'd like it if everything could go on like it was.

You mean not tell Mum?

Do we have to?

But then you'd have something you could never say.

I've got a stomach ache.

I don't care if she goes crazy.

So long as it's you she goes crazy with.

I can tell her to leave you alone because I'm your mum.

I don't think that works.

FIRED

You shouldn't fire people by email.

You can't come bursting in here and shouting.

I'm just saying it needs to be face to face.

I'm sorry, I do appreciate, but I'm busy at the moment, if you could

I need to be looked in the eye and you say you're firing me

redundancy isn't

just say it to my face, you're fired, just say it, you're a coward you can't say it

why don't you speak to my p.a. and make an appointment

just say it, you're fired, just say it

MESSAGE

It's a message

killing people

yes because then they understand

killing yourself

they understand what you're telling them

but they don't do they, they just

because the deaths show how important it is

no they just say you're a terrorist or

and the terror is a message

but they don't get it do they, they just pass laws and lock people up and

if enough people did it because they don't really feel terror do they, they don't live in terror, if they lived in terror they'd be getting the message.

Would you do it yourself?

I don't think I would, no.

Because you're scared?

I don't think that message is what I want to say.

GRASS

What did you do that for?

I thought

What do you think's going to happen to you?

I know but

and to me and the children did you think about that?

It seemed like the right thing to do.

So will we have to change who we are and go and live somewhere else?

I didn't say

and you'll be a protected witness and all our life we'll be living in fear in a mobile home in a desert in America?

I didn't say who I was, I just made the phone call

from your own phone?

no of course not from my own phone, I'm not stupid

well you are but ok, from a public

yes of course

but near here like in the high street

no I took a train

you took a train? when?

today, to make the call, I went to Brighton

why Brighton?

I don't know, it's somewhere you can go quickly on a train

so you didn't go to work? You weren't at work you could've got the kids from school

I was in Brighton

I'd have liked a day out in Brighton

it wasn't a day out in Brighton, I made the call on a public phone in Brighton, I had a coffee and I got the train back.

And what did you say?

I just gave them the name, I said this is the person you want in connection with, no I won't give my name thank you, goodbye. That's all.

But if they know the call came from Brighton and they could find out who knew him who went to Brighton

they won't do that, they don't need to know who I am, they just need to know who to look at but if he finds out you went to Brighton

but he's not going to know what I did in Brighton

you can't be sure of that, what if he's got a mate in the police who says we got a tip it was you, it came from Brighton, and someone else tells him they saw you get on a train to go to Brighton

how likely is that? why would he have a mate in the police? of course he doesn't have a mate in the police, do I have a mate in the police, you're making a whole thing up that's not going to happen.

I don't see why you had to do it.

It wasn't very nice what he did, was it.

He's a friend of yours.

He's not a friend of mine.

He's not now. He doesn't know he's not now, what if you see him? what if I see him? what if he comes round here and says the police are on to me what am I going to do can you help me?

You're making things up again.

No I'm not. That's what's going to happen.

TERMINAL

Doctor, one thing before I go. Can you tell me how long I've got?

There's not an exact answer to that.

I'd be grateful for anything you can give me an idea.

Well let me say ten per cent of people with this condition are still alive after three years.

That's helpful, thank you.

3

SCHIZOPHRENIC

How do you know I'm evil?

I've been told it.

Who by? Who by?

You know the traffic lights at the corner?

yes

i'm getting signals. The ones on the left as you go up from here.

Ok and what do they say?

I won't tell you.

Why not?

Because it's about you, it's what you're like, and you know that yourself I'm not going to say it.

Do they tell you to hurt people?

Not people. You.

But you know when you take your medication that doesn't happen.

That's why I stopped because it was making it hard to get the information.

You do know you're ill.

I've been told that.

SPIES

So we went to war on a completely

yes but how were they to know

they did know, they knew, he'd already admitted it wasn't true

he said it to the Germans

and the CIA knew

but Bush and Blair didn't know

didn't want to know

they had to rely

they wanted it to be true

they thought it was true, everyone thought

not everyone no, plenty of people, I didn't, I always knew it wasn't true

you can't have known

I knew it was all made-up stuff

and how did you know?

because of what America's like, what it wanted to do

you didn't know it was made up, you wanted it to be made up, that's what you wanted to be true.

And it turns out I was right, didn't it.

Do you think you've just won an argument?

DREAM

I had this dream last night, I was in a garden and there were blackberries, big bushes of brambles, I was picking them, and a butterfly flew across and I could see this orange-and-black butterfly really clearly on a yellow rose, but then the whole thing was a dance because I was at the ballet. And I looked all those things up on a website about dreams, blackberry, butterfly, ballet, and every single one means infidelity. So now I know he's cheating.

So you don't feel you have to be faithful to him any more?

No, why should I?

So that leaves the way clear for us?

Don't you think?

Unless it's not about him.

Who then?

You. You and me.

That would mean we're definitely going to do it.

So either way.

Either way.

RECLUSE

Two inside, one outside the door who can be heard.

Don't answer

it's only

look through the spyhole.

You're right, I thought it was the boy delivering the

don't answer don't

of course I won't answer, don't panic.

Hello. Hello Mr Rushmore. I believe this is where you live. We saw you going in, we know the car outside is

make him go away

shall I speak to him?

yes no no

and of course I respect your desire for privacy and it would so much help your thousands of admirers to understand if you could say a few words to us about that privacy about how it feels to live here in a forest miles from

I'm going to die

sh it's all right

five minutes of your time I could explain to the world why you've chosen to leave it all behind and withdraw to this remote

I should have a gun

because that would enable you to set the record straight about your ex-wife's allegations of

I'm going to bed

to confirm or deny that you said of the Queen that she

I'll have to hide in the cupboard

to put an end to speculation once and for all about your

I'd kill myself but they'd write an obituary

shall I tell him to

no no because then they'll write about you

it doesn't matter

it does they mustn't if they know about you if you talk to them I'll never see you again

because we have a photograph of you taken last week in the

why don't I just

ALL RIGHT.

What?

Hello, Mr Rushmore?

I have three things to say. I am now a citizen of China. I have six illegitimate children. I have recently been abducted by aliens and returned to earth unharmed.

Mr Rushmore, if you could just open the door for a moment

that's all right you see that's fine if I tell him lies that's fine I haven't told them anything about myself at all that's fine I feel fine about that I think that's fine I think I feel fine about

and when exactly were you last in China?

that's fine that's fine

good good I'm glad you feel ok about

and will he go away now?

in a while he's sure to go away in a while if we keep

Mr Rushmore

Time passes.

He's gone.

He's gone.

Well that's all right then

yes

you handled that very

no I feel

what?

I feel terrible I feel

but you didn't tell him

but he knows

he doesn't know anything it was lies

he knows I'm the person that told those lies

no because he doesn't know it was lies

yes but he knows I said

you mean he'll work out it's lies and

whichever whichever he knows I said those words he knows I
was in this room we'll have to move he knows it was me he
knows I shouted out those

so you don't feel as good as you

no no I don't I feel

GOD'S VOICE

God told you to do it?

He did, yes.

How?

How do you mean, how?

Did you hear words?

It was the word of God.

But like something you could hear with your ears, actual words
from outside you?

They came into me.

The words.

What God said.

So you didn't exactly hear…?

In my heart.

So how does that work then?

I was praying about it

in words?

sometimes in words, sometimes just

silently

the words were silent, I was praying in

in your head

if you like, my head my heart

so sometimes in words and sometimes

sometimes just being in a state where I was praying

I don't know what state that is

well you'll have to take it from me there is such a state

ok, so there you are praying

praying and not knowing, seeking guidance, open to guidance from God

ok

and he told me what to do.

What's his voice like?

Firm. Kind.

He speaks English?

What sort of a question is that?

I know but does he speak rp or have a regional accent? I'm trying to understand what you heard.

It wasn't hearing like I hear you but it was hearing.

And he definitely said do it.

He said do it.

In words.

In words and inside me in knowing it was the right thing to do.

In your heart?

Right through my whole being.

In your toes?

Yes in my toes, will you stop now?

THE CHILD WHO DIDN'T KNOW FEAR

One person tells a story to another.

Once upon a time there was a child who didn't know what fear was and he wanted to find out. So his friends said, Cold shiver down your back, legs go funny, sometimes your hands no not your hands yes your hands tingle, it's more in your head, it's in your stomach, your belly you shit yourself, you can't breathe, your skin your skin creeps, it's a shiver a shudder do you really not know what it is? And the child said, I don't know what you mean. So they took him to a big dark empty house everyone said was haunted. They said, No one's ever been able to stay here till morning, you won't stay till midnight, you won't last a hour, and the child said, Why, what's going to happen? And they said, You'll know what we mean about being frightened. And the child said, Good, that's what I want to know. So in the morning his friends came back and there was the child sitting in the dusty room. And they said, You're still here? what happened? And the child said, There were things walking about, dead things, some of them didn't have heads and a monster with glowing – and his friends said, Didn't you run away? and the child said, There were weird noises like screams and like music but not music, and his friends said, What did you feel? and the child said, It came right up to me and put out its hand, and his friends said, Didn't your hair your stomach the back of your neck your legs weren't you frightened? And the child said, No, it's no good, I didn't feel anything, I still don't know what fear is. And on the way home he met a lion and the lion ate him.

STAR

It takes the light two point eight million years to get here.

So we're looking at two point eight million years ago.

It might not be there. It could have died by now.

So who's going to see that?

It might not even be people by then. The sun's only eight minutes.

In the morning let's wait eight minutes and see if it's there now.

4

WEDDING VIDEO

Several people.

This is the bit

this is the funny bit watch

where he spills

ah ah ha ha ha

gets me every time

and look look the sweet

and wasn't she little then

just a tiny girl in her pink

and now she's my god you should see

and her boyfriend

have you met him he's the most

and there's that woman

we never knew who she was

yes she's there in the video but who invited

someone who just goes to strangers' weddings

there she is talking to who is that that uncle of yours is it no

and look at the dresses I mean

because now you wouldn't dream

it shows you it's history

yes the children like it because

and the grandchildren are going to

and it can go down in the family and they can see

and all the ones of them as babies and little

and all the ones of their weddings and their

but it's sad we haven't got our grandparents' wedding video

or great great

or everybody that ever lived videos of

Henry the Eighth

Jesus walking on the

no further back if we had cave if we had Neanderthal

and dinosaurs

but who'd be working the camera?

and things coming out of the sea and tiny specks

then we'd know we'd know

we could keep

we'd know what

because I wouldn't remember all this if without the video I
wouldn't remember hardly anything at all about it because I
can't remember anything about that day that's not on the video
not clearly

I can remember putting the ring

no I can't see that in my mind's

and someone was sick

oh look it's the speeches now listen to Dad's speech it's so

SAVANT

What did you have for lunch on October the third 1998?

Chicken soup and a salad. I was at home. I had the chicken soup in a blue bowl. The salad had tomatoes, lettuce and chicory but no onion because I didn't want my breath to smell of onion when I went to the movies with my brother in the afternoon. The movie began at 2.15.

What was the movie?

Godzilla.

What happened in it?

You want the whole thing? Shot by shot?

Can you do that?

Let's not do that.

Ok. I remember Godzilla. There's a lizard that's been irradiated by a nuclear explosion so it's a monster and it goes to New York and the American military drops bombs on it.

That's the one.

What did you do afterwards?

We walked back to my brother's place and had poached eggs on toast. I had two cups of tea in his red mug, the one with a chip.

What was the weather like?

Rain in the morning but it cleared up. Rain in the evening. Rain the next morning.

June the sixth 2004.

EX

I'm glad we've done it, just to see

so am I

after all these years

because it was very important at the time, it's been very important

it has for me, all my life, very important

so never to have seen each other again would have been

it would have been impossible

it would have been sad anyway.

You remember the Italian restaurant?

no, yes, on the corner was it?

with the bushes outside?

no, I'm mixing it up with

I can see the waiter now

no, I can't get the waiter

the waiter with the moustache who always smiled so much when we came in.

I used to have spaghetti carbonara and you had vongole.

I can't remember eating, no, I was too busy looking at you probably.

I really loved you then.

I loved you.

I always remember you standing in that field

I wonder where that was, was it

all the buttercups.

I've got a really clear picture of you running ahead of me down a street. We were running for a bus I think.

Do you remember that hotel, we took a room for a couple of hours in a hotel, there was green wallpaper and we stood there kissing.

I remember the first time

no, that's got overlaid by so many other times, I can't, I remember once by a river, we were practically on a public footpath

the kitchen, the kitchen at your friend's house

which friend?

I never knew your friends' names

was it Chris? Terry?

I don't know, you remember the kitchen?

I might if I knew which house. Did we do it in a kitchen?

Behind the door. There was soup on the cooker.

I remember us just looking at each other.

The time in the street, we just stopped.

I was thinking more a time when you were sitting on the side of the bed.

Was that early on or near the end?

Near the end I think. Do you know the time I mean?

I sometimes go past that coffee shop.

Which one?

The one where we kept trying to say goodbye.

I think I've blotted that whole day out.

We were really happy.

Or sad, we used to cry.

Did we?

Sometimes.

MEMORY HOUSE

to improve my mind

no but you've got a good

my memory to improve

forget a lot?

not not

like names

like names like faces

we all

yes but

not worth worrying

but I want to learn

ah

huge amount of memorising

of course

vocabulary

yes

statistics

statistics

every imaginable

I see your point

stacks of information which I have to

somehow

somehow acquire and retain.

So how do you intend

this course this memory

to improve your

lists lists as exercises

like getting the muscles

muscles of the brain

which of course I know it doesn't have muscles

and more than that a technique

for remembering

ancient ancient technique Romans

didn't know they

and all sorts Renaissance

they had a lot of brains then in the

Leonardo da Vinci

so did he?

I don't know that he actually did

not this technique

not necessarily this actual technique

though he might have done

it's beside the point, the point

the actual technique

the actual technique is you take a place like you could take a house

take a house?

in your mind this is a mental take a house you know in your mind

like my aunt's got a house

there you are take this house in your mind and you've got a list of things you want to remember like what?

like anything like this list I've got here this exercise

crocodile pincushion

and you go round the house in your mind you go round and you put something in each room

can't quite remember all the rooms because

can't remember the rooms?

in my aunt's house I've never

take where you live

only be able to remember three things

no you could go round the room and put one on the table and one on the chair

oh I see

but you'll have to remember what order

what order I'm going round the room

is that all right?

yes I could do that.

So I've got my house when I was a child in my mind and I'm going to go round it now and put a crocodile on the doorstep

a crocodile on the table

a pincushion just inside on the mat

pincushion on the chair

pair of scissors in the sittingroom on the sofa

pair of scissors on the other chair

axe in the diningroom on the table

axe on the other chair

wristwatch

wristwatch

could you just in your head do you mind I can't

I'm not bothered by hearing yours

keep seeing your room in my

because I don't know where you lived as a child so it doesn't

so I can still say

yes if it helps and I'll just

thank you ok so wristwatch in the kitchen on the cooker
elephant on the stairs poundcoin in the bathroom biro on their
bed hedgehog on my bed tree in the attic

tree

makes ten. So now we go round

pick them up

on the doorstep crocodile

crocodile pincushion

pincushion yes scissors in the sittingroom

scissors wristwatch

no not yet

oh it's on the other

sh

so it's

axe

axe axe wristwatch

wristwatch

elephant

poundcoin

now where did I put?

oh

what?

bedroom

on top of the cd player

no in the bedroom I suddenly

biro

yes of course biro but I suddenly

what

saw my father

in his bedroom

my father getting dressed

he's not he wasn't

no it's nothing

nothing awful happened you're not remembering

no nothing like that at all I just suddenly saw him and

so when did you last

no it's just that he's dead and I don't

of course years ago I'd forgotten I'm

no it's nothing it's just he was there in the bedroom

and that's a memory is it

yes I suppose it is of course it's a memory from

from when you were little

yes because he's very I'm only half his size so

so is this like a new

yes a new memory and I'm seeing

you can see with your eyes when you were

say maybe four and the sunlight

sunlight

yes because it's sunny in the room shining in behind him and on the floor on my feet

you can see your feet

I can see my feet when I was four

which isn't a memory you've always

no I've never

and you're sure it's not some horrible

some repressed no it's not it's just a memory isn't it

so the room faced east

yes it's morning in the room and I just saw it

some sort of crossed wire.

Because of course it's biro

biro

hedgehog

I've lost the hedgehog wait oh it's in the microwave I don't know where I went next oh I know on the pile of old newspapers it's a tree

tree in the attic.

So could we say the list straight off

I'm sure we could

and then do another list

lots of lists

and how do we keep the lists separate

I'm not sure yet I've got to

because I'll keep getting the hedgehog in the microwave

wait a minute I'll find out

find out what to do next.

DINNER

I did tell you

you didn't

I did I said Wednesday we're going to dinner with

but you didn't

yes because I remember because you said

all right I must have forgotten I'm sorry

yes you did

I'm sorry.

PIANO

Three people.

This is Jennifer.

Hello, Jennifer.

Here's the piano. You can play the piano.

I've never played the piano.

You sit here.

He sits. He plays well and JENNIFER *sings. He gets up.*

Hello.

This is Jennifer.

Hello, Jennifer.

FLASHBACK

Breathe

ah ah ah

just breathe

ah ah

I've got you, it's all right

ah

all right.

Thank you. Sorry. I keep seeing… I can see… I can't stop seeing…

I wish I could stop it for you.

Short of smashing in my skull.

They say time, you may be able to forget, even if it's a long time.

Once it's in there. Once you know that stuff.

5

LINGUIST

How many languages do you know?

To speak fluently

or a bit

well of course some languages I only know a few words, while others

take something like a table, take a table, how many languages can you

table table trapezi stol mesa meza tarang tabulka

That's so fantastic. Tabulka. Meza. They all mean table.

They all mean the same thing as each other.

Table.

Table means the same thing.

Yes, they all mean table.

Or they all mean meza.

Oh if you mean Chinese.

Or in fact Swahili.

I can't help feeling it actually is a table.

MATHS

I don't want to spend an evening with them again.

You like them. You like her.

He will keep making his point about mathematics not corresponding to reality because it's just a system our brains developed as we evolved in the world and we've had that argument.

Whereas maths is really true.

Yes.

Which is why if an equation wouldn't work without there being an infinite number of universes there really must be an infinite number of universes.

That sort of thing.

But we do only have our senses, don't we, to perceive with and maybe there's all sorts of other things we haven't evolved to perceive. Like an earthworm can't know about flying or a bird can't know about computers.

Don't let's have this conversation.

Why not go and see them and keep off the topic? We can argue about politics.

Because he won't keep off the topic, he likes trying to make me angry because he fancies you. And nobody understands what we're talking about and the evening's ruined and we all get drunk and I feel like shit in the morning and can't work.

Are you saying you never want to see them again?

He says maths is just consistent with itself. He keeps saying it doesn't mean anything.

What does it mean then?

All right, we'll go and see them.

She fancies you.

SEX

What sex evolved to do is get information from two sets of genes so you get offspring that's not identical to you. Otherwise you just keep getting the same thing over and over again like hydra or starfish. So sex essentially is information.

You don't think that while we're doing it do you?

It doesn't hurt to know it. Information and also love.

If you're lucky.

GOD

God gives your life meaning. You've said that.

Yes, so?

If there wasn't God there'd be no meaning to your existence?

And?

So does God have a higher god to give his existence meaning? and that god a higher god and that god

no of course not

of course not, so all this stuff he's done, he might find it all a bit meaningless. I'm surprised he's not depressed.

I don't think he minds whether he means anything or not. I don't think he thinks about it.

So why do you think about it?

I'm not God am I?

But I don't mind not meaning anything, does that make me God?

It makes you really annoying.

RASH

It's just a rash.

But why, why a rash?

There's all kinds of like detergents and animals and stuff in the air. Shall we have him tested?

He's trying to tell us something.

Oh come on.

Or he's trying not to tell us something.

Did you get the new cream?

CHILDREN

You can't have children?

No.

You can't have children?

No.

How did you find that out?

When I was married, it came up, we had tests and it was me.

So was that why?

No of course not.

I thought it was because she went off with the Spaniard.

She did

and she's got a baby now hasn't she, she and the Spaniard have got a bambino.

So it makes a difference does it?

SHRINK

It used to just be pain

the memories of what happened to you when you were a child and

and the things I wasn't letting myself remember of course

the things you'd

yes and now

so the analysis has stopped it hurting

not so much stopped

as what?

changed it into

changed it into?

transformed it

into what though?

It has meaning.

Because you see where it comes from?

partly that

and how it's affected the way you are?

partly that

and partly what?

It just has meaning now.

What does it mean?

It doesn't mean something. There isn't exactly another thing that it means.

Then what do you mean when you say it has meaning now?

You spoil it. You completely spoil everything. You always do.

That must be painful for you. You can take it to your analyst and have it turned into meaning.

6

THE CHILD WHO DIDN'T KNOW SORRY

You have to say you're sorry.

I'm not sorry.

But you know you hurt him. You have to say you're sorry.

I don't feel sorry.

You have to say it.

CLIMATE

I'm frightened.

Just walk instead of driving and don't take so many hot baths.

I'm frightened for the children.

There were those emails those scientists, I can't remember the detail

no it didn't make any difference in the end

no I think you're right, most scientists all agree it's a catastrophe. The question is how bad a catastrophe.

It's whether they drown or starve or get killed in the fights for water.

I'd choose drowning.

Are you really not going to take it seriously?

I don't know how to.

I don't know how to.

CENSOR

Page forty-two.

Page forty-two.

The sentence beginning 'On the 21st of May...'

Yes, I've got it.

I'm afraid that's going to have to go.

Why is that?

The Ministry of Defence considers it a breach of security.

It's not classified information.

That is nevertheless their view.

Have you got a lot of these?

About thirty.

Let's hear the next one then.

WIFE

But I am your wife.

You look like my wife.

That's because I am. Look, even that little birthmark behind my ear. Look.

Yes, I see it.

It's me. Darling sweet, it's me. I'm here.

No, she's gone. They've all gone.

Who's gone?

Everyone I know. Everyone who loved me.

No, I love you.

I don't want you to love me, I don't know you.

There's things only we know, aren't there. That day on the beach with the shells. You remember that?

Yes, of course.

And cabbages. Why is cabbages a funny word, we're the only ones who have cabbages as a joke because of what happened with the cabbages. Cabbages is a joke, yes?

Cabbages was a joke I shared with my wife. I miss my wife.

But I am… Let me touch you. If you'd see what it feels like to touch me. If we made love you'd know it was me because there are things we like to do and no one else would know that, if I was a stranger pretending to be her I wouldn't know those things, you'd feel you were back with me, you would I know, please.

You disgust me. You frighten me. What are you?

DECISION

I've written down all the reasons to leave the country and all the reasons to stay.

So how does that work out?

There's things on both sides.

How do you feel about it?

No, I'm trying to make a rational decision based on the facts.

Do you want me to decide for you?

Based on what? The facts don't add up.

I'd rather you stayed here. Does that help?

THE CHILD WHO DIDN'T KNOW PAIN

But what is it?

Pain is pain, it's just

if I pinch

aah, get off. But if I pinch you

nothing

nothing at all

but stop because I get bruises.

How come you don't

I never did when I was a baby

you were born like

yes and I used to chew my fingers

you mean chew?

and they got bandages put over or I'd chew them to the bone
because you know how babies

put everything in their mouth

I'd put myself in my mouth because it wasn't any different.

And if you fell down

I threw myself down

because it didn't hurt

jumped down a whole flight of stairs because that was a quick
way

and you were all right

broke both my legs and once when I went swimming there were
rocks under the water and when I came out my legs were
pouring blood because I hadn't felt

so you can't feel anything

emotions I feel feelings

but physical

not pain, no.

And why not?

because there's no signal going up to my brain

from your legs

from anywhere to my brain to say there's damage, it's hurting

so you never know what hurting is

so tell me what it's like.

Hurting is well it's pain, it's like uncomfortable but more, it's something you'd want to move away from but you can't, it's an intense sensation, it's hard to ignore it, it's very

but why would you mind that?

because it hurts. But no, sometimes pain's all right if it's not bad like if your gum's sore and you keep poking it with your tongue or you might cut your finger and you hardly notice, yes if you're doing something exciting, soldiers can lose a leg and not even know it

that's like me

yes but they know it afterwards. And bad pain

yes but why, what is it?

if someone's tortured if they give them electric shocks it's unbearable or if they've got cancer sometimes they want to die because my uncle

yes but I still don't know what it is about pain

it's just pain

but what is it?

You've been unhappy?

yes

if someone you love doesn't love you, you thought they loved
you and they don't

yes

or you've done something you wish you hadn't done it's too late
now and you've hurt someone and there's nothing you can do to
put it right

yes

does that help?

So it's like being unhappy but in your leg?

But it's also just what it is, like red is red and blue is blue.

But red isn't red, it's waves and it's red to us.

So there you are, that's what it's like.

Can I pinch you again?

EARTHQUAKE

Have you seen the earthquake? There's this building my god
you think things are solid but they just break.

Yes I've seen it.

Imagine being in it, imagine you're lying on your back and
there's this wall a few inches above your face and you can't sit
up even an inch and if you do it might come down on you. And
the air running out, you keep trying to get a deep breath but
you can't breathe deeply enough because very soon there's
going to be no more oxygen. And if you were injured if you're
in pain while all that's going on and where are your family are
they dead or in agony and will anyone come to get you out and
how many hours or days, I'm just so upset by it.

I wouldn't want to be in it obviously, poor them of course. I
mean I do know about it.

But you don't care.

I can't say I feel it, no. You really feel it?

I cried. Of course I feel it. I cried.

Ok.

And imagine the wave coming, imagine hearing it coming and running away and you can't get away, it came so fast did you see how fast it came?

Yes, I saw it.

You're not upset though.

That black wave with the cars in it was awesome.

7

CHINESE POETRY

'The girl waits at the door of her house on the mountain.'

What it literally says is 'mountain girl door'.

So maybe

A girl from the mountain is waiting outside my door. A girl climbs the mountain and comes to a door.

To get the girl you have to go through a door into the mountain.

The mountain is a door only a girl can open.

The girl's as big as a mountain and can't get through the door.

What's the next line?

MANIC

My god, look at that flower, thank you so much, have you ever seen such a red, red is blood and bullfights and seeing red is anger but red is joyful, red is celebration,

yes, I like it

in China red is lucky how lucky we are to have red flowers,

shall I get a vase?

in China white is death and here black is death but ghosts are white of course so a chessboard is death against death, and blood of course could be death but it's lifeblood isn't it, if you look at the flower it's so astounding

yes

it means so much to me that you gave me red flowers because red is so significant don't you think? it means stop and of course it means go because it's the colour of energy and red cars have the most accidents because people are excited by red or people who are already excited like to have red, I'd like to have red, I'll buy a red car this afternoon and we can go for a drive, we can go right up through the whole country don't you think, we can go to Scotland we can go to John o' Groats, did he eat a lot of porridge do you think? but we don't have to start from Land's End or Land's Beginning we should say if we start from there but we won't we'll start from here because here is always the place we start from, isn't that funny, and I need to drive along all the roads in the country because I have to see to the traffic because there are too many cars as everyone knows but our car won't be one too many you'll be quite safe, we'll make sure it's all flowing smoothly in every direction because cars do go in every direction possible and everything goes in every possible direction, so we'll find a vase for the flowers,

yes

I think a green vase because of the primary colours and if they were blue I'd put them in an orange vase and if they were yellow I'd put them in a purple vase, yellow and purple is Easter of course so that's why crocuses, and red and green is Christmas which isn't right now of course it's the wrong time of year, I might have to sort that out when I've got a minute.

GRIEF

Are you sleeping?

I wake up early but that's all right in the summer.

Eating?

Oh enough. Don't fuss.

I've never had someone die.

I'm sorry, I've nothing to say. Nothing seems very interesting.

He must have meant everything to you.

Maybe. We'll see.

FATE

I'm just saying you've got no choice

I have

you have of course you feel as if you have

I have got a choice

you've got a choice but you've no choice about what that choice is, you'll make whichever choice

whichever choice I want

whichever choice you want but you'll want what you want because you have to want what

I don't have to want

you do because of what you're like, that's what what you're like means that you're going to want what you want, because there's your genes and everything that's happened to you and everything else that's happening and all that stuff makes your brain be like that

like what?

like it is

what's it like?

I don't know of course I don't know nobody knows, but if someone could have that information they'd know exactly what you were going to

they can't know

you're crying about it now

I'm not

I knew you would.

But there's random

oh there's random

there's random particles you can't

if you think you're like a random particle

no but

if you think you're a random particle just fizzing

but you can't predict even where

if you think free will is a random particle there's nothing very noble

I didn't say noble

so what is free will if it's not what you're like?

No one could possibly have all that information.

No, of course not.

So maybe that's all right.

I think it's fine. But it does change how you feel, don't you think?

I feel a bit funny

yes you feel as if you're hurtling

hurtling through my life

like the front seat of a roller-coast

but I feel like I'm choosing

yes of course

but I feel like I'm in the front seat of a roller-coaster.

STONE

He's got a special stone.

Is that what he's holding?

Yes he's always got it in his hand.

I know he's always holding

never puts it down

have you seen it?

saw it once

how

made him open his

shall we get it?

I think he needs it

yes shall we get it?

They get the stone and throw it away.

Go and get it then

it's over there

will he know which one?

he can get another one

he might want that one

shall we get him one?

Here have a stone

have another stone

have a stone

Throwing them.

VIRTUAL

I don't care what you say

no but listen

I've never felt like this

that's not the point what you feel

it's the only

because she doesn't exist

I'm not listening.

She doesn't

have you seen her?

yes I've seen her but she doesn't

have you talked to her?

I don't want to talk to

then what do you know about it?

she's not a real

so?

so you admit she's not

she exists she still exists

fine all right she exists but so does your shoe or a can of

you're saying she's no different than a shoe?

she's got no more feelings than

what do you know about

she's a thing she's a thing.

Look I appreciate your concern but just

look

she's beautiful she's intelligent she understands me

she doesn't understand you

she listens to me she likes my poems she's the only

doesn't understand any

she reads my mind she's sensitive to my every

but she's virtual

so?

so she's not

I can't believe just because someone's not flesh and blood you'd

she's just information

and what are you if you're not

yes I know we're

so we're information our genes our

yes but she hasn't

what?

hasn't got an inside to her mind she's not conscious she can't

how do you know she

she's a computer she's a computer game she's not

and can you tell that from what she says?

I don't need to

but can you tell

because she can't

she might and how could she prove it because you wouldn't
believe

I certainly wouldn't

because she says she has

what, thoughts

of course thoughts feelings because she's that complicated she
says she loves

she can't possibly

we know people won't understand but we don't care what you

and what about sex

what about

she hasn't got a body

she's got a fantastic

but not a body you can

she's not in this country at the moment

she can't ever

and the sex is great

it's virtual

it's virtual and great

but she never feels

I don't care what you say

no but listen

I've never felt like this about anyone.

SMALL THING

What are you looking at?

A snail.

Is that the same snail?

Yes. I've been looking at it for a while.

And?

I'm just looking at it.

LAST SCENE

FACTS

Who was president of Coca-Cola from nineteen twenty-five to seven?

HB Jones.

What is the smallest village in Central Asia?

Qat.

Where would you see a huish?

In a gnu's fur.

How many diamonds were mined in 1957?

Sixty thousand four hundred and twenty-eight.

Name two traditional ingredients of poulash.

Duck and fennel.

In 1647 what day was the battle of Stoneham?

June the third. Tuesday.

How far is it from here to the quasar d 66?

Three point four billion light years.

What sound does a capercaillie make?

Aaaah.

Who had the longest hair?

Matilda Lucas.

Of?

Brighouse, Connecticut.

What colour is the caterpillar of the brown-haired bat moth?

Pale orange with black stripes.

Do you love me?

Don't do that.

What is the formula that disproves Gödel's theorem?

X bracket a over t minus pi sigma close bracket to the power of ten minus n to the power of minus one squared

What is a plok?

A stringed instrument played by the Larts of the the Gobi Desert

By what name do we usually refer to Oceanus Australensis Picardia?

I do yes I do. Sea anemone.

RANDOM

RANDOM

These things can happen in any section. DEPRESSION *is an essential part of the play. The other random items are optional.*

DEPRESSION

Each of these is a separate random item. Each is said by one person to another who doesn't respond. The characters can be the same each time, or the depressed person can be the same and the others different, or they can all be different.

we could go for a walk it's a beautiful

there's an exhibition of expressionist

chicken tikka masala

programme starts at 6.40 or if you'd rather we could

glass of red or

thinking of taking one of the kittens there's a ginger one or a

maybe you could read them a story tonight or

the difficulty of getting the Israelis and Palestinians to

and he only has two months to live so I thought we could

a fountain of antimatter in the Milky Way that nobody knew

OPTIONAL

SEMAPHORE

MORSE

SIGN LANGUAGE

BIRDSONG

DANCE

FLAGS

PAINTING

Someone has a large canvas and is flicking paint at it.

PIG LATIN

Ancay ouyay eakspay igpay atinlay?

SANTA

Father Christmas lands his sleigh on the roof and comes down the chimney with his big sack of toys and he'll put presents in your stocking

TABLES

Seven sevens are forty-nine, seven eights are fifty-six, seven nines are sixty-three, seven tens are seventy, seven elevens are seventy-seven, seven twelves are eighty-four, seven thirteens are ninety-one

GENES

AGT TCG AGC CCT TGA CTT GAT TGT GCA TAC
CGT GCT TGA GTC ATG TTG CAC AAC TTG TCG
GTC TCA GTA TGC CCG TGA AAT GTA CAT GTC
CGG TCC GAA TCT GAT TGC CCT TTG TGG AAC
TGT GTG GCA TAG CTA GCC TGG GAC CCT TTG
GGC TGC ACT TGA TTG TCA CCA GGT TGT TCT
GTT GAA TCA TGA TCG GAC CCA CGT CGG CTG
GCC GAC TTT GAC CGG AGT GGT TGT ACC TTG
GTC AGG AAT TGA ACG

DOG

Come. Sit. Stay. Come. Good dog. Fetch. Drop it. Fetch. Good dog. Roll over. Good dog. Come. Heel. No. Come.

KEYS

You don't know where I put the car keys, do you?

MAGAZINE

she's lost two stone… he was going to leave her… look, he's coming out of a club with an unnamed blonde…

GOOGLE

There's a train at 4.22 gets in at half-past eight.

TWITTER

He's in the kitchen cooking spaghetti and he's upset about the news from Tripoli.

ZEN

What's the sound of one hand clapping? I've heard that one.

COLD

Someone sneezes.

SILENCE

This can happen more than once, for different lengths of time.

A Nick Hern Book

Love and Information first published as a paperback original in 2012 by
Nick Hern Books Limited, The Glasshouse, 49a Goldhawk Road,
London W12 8QP, in association with the Royal Court Theatre,
London

Cover image: sciencevisuals.com
Cover design: Ned Hoste, 2H

Typeset by Nick Hern Books, London
Printed in Great Britain by CPI Group (UK) Ltd

A CIP catalogue record for this book is available from
the British Library

ISBN   978 1 84842 288 9

RICHARD BEAN
PLAYS THREE